Susan Elston Wallace, Susan Elston Wallace

Ginèvra or The Old Oak Chest

A Christmas Story

Susan Elston Wallace, Susan Elston Wallace

Ginèvra or The Old Oak Chest
A Christmas Story

ISBN/EAN: 9783743417984

Manufactured in Europe, USA, Canada, Australia, Japa

Cover: Foto ©Andreas Hilbeck / pixelio.de

Manufactured and distributed by brebook publishing software
(www.brebook.com)

Susan Elston Wallace, Susan Elston Wallace

Ginèvra or The Old Oak Chest

GINÈVRA

OR

THE OLD OAK CHEST

A CHRISTMAS STORY

BY

SUSAN E. WALLACE

WITH ILLUSTRATIONS BY

GENERAL LEW WALLACE

NEW YORK

THE H. W. HAGEMANN PUBLISHING COMPANY

114 FIFTH AVENUE

1894

TO

MY BELOVED NIECES,

WHOSE INTEREST IN THIS STORY

SUGGESTED TO THEIR AUNT

THE IDEA OF

TELLING IT TO OTHER CHILDREN.

S. E. W.

CRAWFORDSVILLE, INDIANA,
Christmas, 1880.

HRISTMAS stories are usually merry; and in this happy time, with its shining presents, its good things to eat and to drink, its music, lights, and visitors, all should be gay. But mine must be a sad story, because, being a true one, I cannot change it—one of the saddest of the thousands told since that first Christmas Eve when the traveling star from the East stood still in the midnight above the holy hill of Bethlehem. At Modena you may see the portrait of the lady I tell of; in Florence—rich and glorious city—you will learn her history; and at Abbotsford they show the bridal-chest where Death lay waiting in the dark to claim her as his own.

GINEVRA;

OR,

THE OLD OAK CHEST.

"'Tis an old tale and often told."—*Scott.*

CHAPTER I.

 ANY years ago there lived in an ancient castle in England a proud Baron, who had one child, Ginevra, a little girl named for her mother, who died the night her baby was born.

The servants used to say the Baroness had led a wretched life ; that her lord was harsh and stern at home, as he was fierce and cruel in war ; but this I do not truly know. He dearly loved his little daughter, and hours at a time would carry her in his arms and walk up and down the hall before the blazing fires in winter. It was a fair sight to see the Baron with the baby, in her long white dress, lying on his shoulder, her light hair against his rough beard, or to see him dandle her in his hand, hard almost as the steel gloves he wore to battle, as if she were no more than a feather's weight.

The castle was gloomy and strong, with towers guarded by sentinels, and was enclosed by a high wall of stone, beyond which was a deep moat filled with water, that could be crossed by only one drawbridge.

Once, when there was war in the land, the King called on all good men for help ; and the Baron, ready for battle, gathered his people in the courtyard to hear his last orders. He held up his sword, dinted by many a blow in bloody fight, showed the cross on its hilt, and spoke in a loud voice :

"Swear by this blessed sign, whatever befall, you will defend Lady Ginevra to the death !"

And every man lifted his right hand, knelt where he stood, and swore by the Holy Cross he would defend the Lady Ginevra to the death. He then mounted his coal-black steed, took the baby from her nurse, and lifted her in sight of all the crowd. She clapped her hands and laughed to see the flashing armor and flags embroidered with red roses, and the air rung with the shout : "Long live the Lady Ginevra !"

A fortune-teller had said Ginevra was doomed to sorrow ; and

this made the Baron watch her with anxious care. There was one soldier whose only duty was to guard his young mistress. Said the Baron to him : " Keep her always in sight, Ban. While thou wearest that scar on thy brow, I will remember thou hast saved my life. Some day thou mayest save hers. She is the last of my name and house, and if evil come upon her, my heart will break. Thou art my truest follower, Ban. Whatever else fail, never lose sight of Lady Ginevra."

" I will die ere a hair of her head suffer," said the old retainer, stoutly. " A soldier's scars are his honors, and I will be proud to wear one for my Lady's sake."

So Ban, with spear and sword, was always in sight of his young mistress ; and at night he lay in the corridor, outside her chamber door, his spear against the wall, so that no one could go out or in without waking him.

The Baron fought well for king and country, and at Christmas rode home on his coal-black steed. Then there was a mighty feast in the great hall, and, for two days and nights, whoever chose could eat and drink of the best

The ladies' hall was wreathed with evergreens ; red berries of holly shone bright on the old oak wall, and from the center of the ceiling hung a heavy branch of mistletoe; and every one who passed under it was sure to be caught and kissed. Plates were laid for a hundred guests, and there were oxen roasted whole, and huge pies of venison ; and all night long was heard the sound of harp and horn, and tread of dancers, dancing in tune. Oh! it was a rousing Christmas, and little Ginevra was the soul and life of it all !

There were few books in those days, and instead of reading, she was taught to embroider with silks, to play on the lute, and to sing. She was so gentle and gracious, even the bees, the birds, and the swans on the lake, knew her, and everything that knew her loved her. So watched, and so beloved, fifteen years Ginevra grew,—

> "Fair as a star when only one
> Is shining in the sky."

And the fame of her beauty spread far and wide.

A tranquil life she lived, rarely going beyond the castle, yet loved by many who had children of their own, but who freely spoke of Ginevra as best and dearest where all were near and dear.

"Why, my darling," said the Baron, "why does everybody love my child ?"

"I do not know," she answered, with a thoughtful, puzzled

look. "Perhaps," she added shyly, "it is because I love every-body."

"That much nearer heaven than I," said the father, gazing into the picture-like face, with the mild look which never came into his own except for her. "The angels in heaven can do no more."

Her fresh, light rooms, the only cheerful ones in the dismal stone pile, opened out on a broad balcony, filled with plants; fluttering leaves, speckled shadows, sweet-smelling flowers, through which the sun at setting poured his last, last rays, as lingering through the late twilight to kiss her pure forehead once more. The blessed sunlight! You might think some of its brightness was tangled in the golden head which glanced among the flowers, and that their sweetness had passed into her soul.

It was the Baron's study to smooth from her path every care and trial, and to temper every wind that blew past her. The walls round the courtyard below the balcony were so high it was sheltered from the coldest blasts, so that birds sang in the bare, leafless thickets of shrubbery as though it were always spring; and all the year round it was a delightful playground.

In summer, with her little maid, Geta, she used to play hide and seek in the alleys of the rose garden, where the roses were all red—the Baron would not have a white one among them—and as the quick color came and went in her face, he would say :

" My child, the roses are ever at war in thy cheek."

" Yes, father ; but thou sayest the red always wins."

" So it does, dear heart, and so it shall. No white leaf for us ! The red rose forever ! When I miss it from thy face the sweetness of my life is gone ; and thou must wear one for me ever in thy hair."

Near the castle wall was a dark forest, of which awful tales were told ; how it was full of robber caves, and dens, and dim paths leading into snares and pitfalls, and among roaring wild beasts that were forever seeking what they might devour.

The sentinel on the bridge said he would rather fight the infidel all day than venture into the forest after sundown. Close to its edge, in the shade of giant oaks, was a fountain of marble, with water playing night and day, cold as ice, clear as glass. And here, one summer afternoon, Ginevra strayed with Geta. Her feet scarcely bent the daisies in her path ; the breeze tossed her flossy locks, where the red rose shone like a jewel ; and, as old Ban stalked behind her, like a tall black shadow, he thought he had never seen his Lady so lovely.

When they reached the fountain, Geta tried to tune the lute, but could not play till Ginevra brought the silver strings together; and, as she touched its chords, a fierce stag-hound sprang out of the forest so suddenly, she dropped the lute and screamed for fear.

Quick as lightning, Ban was before her, and in another moment would have split the dog's skull, but a voice shouted:

"Stay! Stay! He will not harm any one!"

Ban stood still, but lowered not his lance. Presently, a youth, mounted on a milk-white steed, rode up, called the hound to his feet, gave his horse's bridle to a page, who followed on a red roan, and then he knelt before Ginevra and quieted her fears.

I do not know how it came to pass, but these four were soon talking as if they had been friends all their days, and there was nothing in the wide world but their own innocent young hearts. They tried their fortune by dropping bay-leaves in the water. Then they sat on mossy roots, and Ginevra sang of the lady who was heartbroken and drowned herself in the fountain for her own true love; and how her spirit rises and floats in the air above it like a mist at evening.

"Thy song is too sad, Lady," said the youth. "Let me have the lute."

With a free hand, he struck the strings, and sang of King

Arthur and his bold knights, and of the daring deeds they did,
whose like England has never seen since his time ; no, nor never
will, till Arthur comes again.   Then he turned his eyes—steel-
blue eyes, flashing like a sword-blade— toward Ginevra, and sang
of love in such strain she thought the fountain stopped its splash-
ing and the trees bent their heads to listen.   When the last echo
of his voice died away, Ban spoke out, and said :

"My Lady, an' it please you, my lord, the Baron has forbidden
us to stay outside the wall after nightfall."

"But, Ban, he knows thou art between me and danger.   Still,
the forest's shades grow dark, and I see thou art right.   The sun
is nearly set."

Then the youth whispered something in her ear, and Ginevra,
blushing brightly, said :

"Never, never !

"Give me a favor to wear—the rose from thy hair, sweet lady.
I, too, belong to the house and banner of the red."

She loosed it from her shining tresses ; he kissed the flower,
put it in his bosom, and said :

"I would not give one of the least of these leaves for the King's
crown."

Lightly he sprung to the saddle, without so much as touching his horse's neck, lifted his plumed cap, and, followed by the page, on the red roan, dashed away into the forest. Ginevra and Geta watched them disappear among the black shadows, and then turned and sighed, they knew not why.

The Baron met them outside the castle gate.

" Where hast thou been, my child?" he asked.

" By Edith's fountain, father."

" And didst thou drop thy rose in it?"

" No; I gave it to a youth who begged it," she answered, blushing.

" Ha! And thou hast brought back two," he said, "and they are both for me, my summer child."

And he kissed her on each cheek.

The color ran up to her forehead, and as she stood in the rosy sunset, with downcast eyes, in the bloom and glow of youth so beautiful, the old Baron's heart yearned toward his daughter. He gathered her in his arms, and said :

" I will carry thee home, little one. Thou art my Rose of the World ; for there is none on earth like thee. As we go, thou shalt tell me of this youth. Did he ride a milk-white steed?"

" Yes ; a high, proud one ; not a single black hair on him ; its mane swam the wind, and its trappings were of scarlet and gold."

" A goodly youth, with spurs ; was he not ? "

" Yes ; his hair was black as the wing of the night raven. He had a noble air, and oh ! an eye that takes your breath ! "

" And his page, Ginevra ? "

" A comely little page, but nothing like his master."

Here Geta made as if she would speak ; her mistress went on :

" But nothing like his master, who carried a bow, a quiver of arrows, and a silver bugle-horn."

" It is young Lord Lovel ! " He was silent a moment. "How old art thou, my daughter ? "

" Sixteen, come Christmas."

Then the Baron fell into a muse, and walked on, carrying her all the way.

After supper he sat beside her in the hall, playing idly with her hand, that was soft as the down on the dove's breast; and at last he said :

" Sweet child, tell me, dost thou know aught of love—young love, I mean, not father's love ? "

"I have sung it in song, and heard it in story," she answered timidly.

"Listen, then. Lord Lovel is thy betrothed. Thou wert promised to him in the cradle; but we fathers have kept the secret, and let true love find its own, as it is certain to do, and has done to-day. On thy sixteenth birthday we will have the betrothal feast. Now go to sleep and dreams that maidens often have ere they reach thy age."

Ginevra's chamber was a lofty room, with curtained bed so high it could be reached only by steps. Geta slept in a cot beside her. They usually fell asleep at dark, and awoke at daybreak, but that night there was no slumber in their eyelids, and the tall clock on the stairs struck midnight ere they ceased to talk of the winsome young lord, and his gallant little page, Alfred.

Turning on the stone floor in the corridor outside, Ban heard the murmur of voices under the door, and the shrewd soldier smiled in the dark, and winked his one eye, as he said to himself:

"That arrow was double-headed. It's all over with my Lady and that forward little Geta."

CHAPTER II.

OUR weeks before the next Christmas the Baron proclaimed there would be good cheer for all comers two days and nights at the castle. And when the time came, the bell on the tower, which sounded only for births, deaths, and weddings, rung merrily through the frosty air, bonfires were lighted on the hills, the fountain ran wine, and every man who chose might put in his cup and drink his fill. Outside the wall were crowds of men gaming, wrestling, and trying their strength, and a few bloody noses and a cracked skull or two; but that was nothing in those rough times.

In the hall were knights and earls wearing belt, spur, and plume; gay ladies in velvets, with sweeping trains; and children pages, and pert maids, who did nothing but stand under the mistletoe; and then what kissing, what blushing, what shouts, what laughter! The sun never shone on so merry a Christmas!

Instead of the red rose, Ginevra wore a coronet of pearls; and in that goodly company her beauty shone like a star, the brightest where ten thousand are.

The ladies' hall was a lordly room, with long rows of columns, wreathed with garlands; and there the guests assembled at night. As they walked together, Ginevra said to Lord Lovel :

"I will give thee a weary chase for me some day. I will frighten thee now."

And, with a bound, she darted from column to column, and was out of sight. Vexed and troubled, Lovel flew after her. He was swift as a deer, but could not overtake her; and in the midst of the chase, she stole behind and touched him on the shoulder, laughing merrily at his fears.

" Promise me, sweetheart," said he, "thou wilt never fly from me again, till thou spread thy white wings for Heaven. Even Ban lost his breath trying to follow thee."

" I will not promise," she said, shaking her sunny ringlets. " I love to tease too well. Ban says my feet have wings, and with them I find hiding-places where no one can follow."

" I fear thou wilt be lost in some of these dark passages ; no one living understands all their windings ; but I'll hide thee next Christmas !"

" Where, my Lord ? In the donjon keep, behind the iron gratings ?"

"A safer place than that. In my heart, sweet love. There I'll shut thee up, and keep thee safe forever and a day."

Then he gave a close kiss, and did not take his eyes off her till it was time to part.

When the night was far spent, a strange minstrel came to the door, and begged to look, if but for one moment, on the Lady Ginevra.

He was old and poor, and shook with cold. Room was made for him by the fire ; and when he had eaten and drank, he lifted his harp, and, moving back from the crowd, passed under the mistletoe. Now, it was a great slight for one to do this and not be kissed, and, of course, nobody wanted to kiss an old beggar. He heard the laugh and jeer, and, looking up, saw the green branch ; then his head sunk on his breast with shame. Ginevra saw it, and snatched an ivy wreath, and stepped toward him, saying playfully,

" Kneel down !"

He knelt and kissed the hem of her robe. Not even she was ever more beautiful than then.

" I crown thy harp, and call thee knight"—she touched his shoulder. " Be thou wise, brave, and tuneful. Rise, Sir Minstrel, and let these lords and ladies hear thy bravest harping."

For a moment the old man was overcome. Then he swept the harp with such skill and grace there was instant silence. He sang :

GINEVRA.

He had heard of her beauty, but the half had not been told ; what his eyes had this night seen would ever be a part of sight ; his hand was weak and old, but so long as he could touch a string it should be to her name ; and at his dying hour thought of her tender pity would warm his heart as it had never warmed with wine.

Praises ran through the crowd ; the Baron sent Alfred with a purse of broad gold pieces, but the minstrel put it back with a smile, and unclasped the ragged cloak; down dropped hood, mask, and gray hair ; out stepped a youth, tall, straight, and handsome; on his neck a sparkling chain the Baron knew right well.

" It is Prince Edward !   Long live the Prince !" he exclaimed.

And every man knelt and shouted, till the arches rang,

" Long live Prince Edward !"

He bowed his thanks, and lightly touched the harp again. His fingers strayed uncertainly among the strings, like one busy with memory; a moment more, and he seemed to catch the

melody, and, resting his burning glance upon Ginevra's fair face,
he sang:

PRINCE EDWARD'S SONG.

" In blinding snow, as wild winds blow,
    I left the forest's gloom,
  And, following sounds that change the night
    To brightness and to bloom,

" I've found where all sweet flowers live,
    Where summer sings and never dies,
  Its roses, Lady, on thy cheek,
    Its violets in thine eyes.

" The harp and sword I bring to thee
    Are not an offering meet;
  With them, my hand and England's crown,
    I lay before thy feet.

" O, Lady, like the evening star,
    Bend to me now or never;
  For I will see thee ne'er again,
    Unless I see thee ever."

Then the Prince led Ginevra to the dance, and it was whis-

pered she was fit to be a queen; but the Baron shook his head,
even in that proud hour, and said:

"She must wed whom she will. I cannot force her heart."

When the holidays were ended, Lovel set off to Holy Land,
to be gone a twelvemonth and a day. Ginevra wept bitterly, but
promised to keep true heart and constant mind till he should
come home, never, day nor night, to leave her more.

The King's son tarried and wooed her with words women love
to hear; but she quietly said:

"I will wed my own true love, or die a nun."

He prayed her to give him a favor, a scarf, a glove, a ring;
but no; she spoke so firmly he saw it was useless to stay longer,
and went away, swearing he would spring into the Thames or
the depths of the sea, and drown himself.

Ginevra watched a splendid train escort him through the forest, and when it was out of sight, said:

"Ban, dost thou think he will kill himself? It would be a sad
thing to lose our Crown Prince."

Ban smiled grimly; he had been a wild one, but was tame
enough now.

"Lady Ginevra," he said, "ever since the world was made,

men have died from time to time, and worms have eaten them, but not for love. Prince Edward's heart is sound ; he will marry in less than a twelvemonth and a day."

And so he did.

Now there were many curious things about this castle which have not been mentioned. In the bell-tower, so high, it seemed to touch the sky, lived a crow, said to be a hundred years old, and an owl that hooted at night, and winked and blinked by day. There were lonesome cells where monks used to live ; narrow corridors and winding ways easy to be lost in ; and secret doors in odd places where you would never think of looking for a door; but Ginevra knew every dark corner from turret to foundation ; in every black closet her bright eyes had peered, and under every hidden archway her fairy feet had glided along.

Looking from the highest tower of the castle, a dim line of heavenly blue marked the Ocean. More than any other view Ginevra loved that. When the day was fine, she could see the curlews and herons in the glancing light, and almost hear their screaming and the lapping of the water among the stones of the pebbly shore. Sometimes it showed as many tints as though the sea-shells from the depths had swum to the surface, opened to the

sun, and floated on the top of the waters like many colored blossoms. And when the sun went down it was a path of gold, a splendor like the pathways of angels. In calm or storm, in leaden sky or roseate light, through every change, Ginevra loved the sea. Ban used to watch her to the top of the tower, and grumble and mutter: "My Lady will come to grief all along of her skipping and racing into strange places. She'll be sorry for it some day."

"Is it so very hard, my good Ban," she would say, laughing at him, "for a strong soldier, who fought in Flanders, to follow one girl over one house?"

And he would bow and smile back again, as he said:

"I was only thinking of my Lady's safe keeping. There's no tiring me. No, no, no! I would march my feet off for her."

So petted and guarded, so gay and full of pleasantness was her life, that every day of the year was happy as a birthday.

The Baron did not worry Ginevra with teachers and grammars. He did not think much of book knowledge, calling it a weariness of the flesh, and a wiser man than any Baron called it that, three thousand years ago. Nor was her nurse allowed to tell her frightful tales, though the old woman liked nothing better than to scare the servants with ghost stories in windy nights. Her

orders were to tell no Christmas stories, except such as the Bible
told; and she used to show a book with pictures of the Holy
Family, the shepherds listening to the angels' songs, heard but
once on earth, and the flight into Egypt. This last was a very
choice engraving of Mary, the Virgin Mother, asleep under a palm-
tree, and baby angels bending back the leaves, smiling sunnily
down on the Divine Child, whose light lightened the bank of lilies
where they lay. Then the nurse would explain how the Mother
of Christ still lives, and is always near motherless children, listening to their prayers and waiting to comfort them. And Ginevra
loved the tale and believed it, and never spoke a word she would
not wish the Holy Mother to hear.

In those good old times people played and laughed more than
we do, and a first-rate story-teller was better thought of than a
fine musician nowadays.

So, with play and needlework, time went on. Knights, earls,
and gentlemen tried to win Ginevra from her vows; but she sent
them away more madly in love than when they came to offer hand
and heart. At the hour when the nightingale sings, minstrels and
lovesick troubadours harped under her lattice; but she kept true
heart and constant mind, and when six months had passed, a

carrier-dove—a tame, fond thing—flew to the balcony, bearing a letter tied around its neck, scaled with red, and stamped with a rose.   It was from Lord Lovel, who wrote he would be home Christmas.

The Baron went to London for her wedding-clothes.   They were rich and rare as any princess's ; her veil was like silver mist ; but nothing was so fine as a pair of slippers of white velvet, embroidered with pearls.   Had you seen them, you would have said they were for some little child.

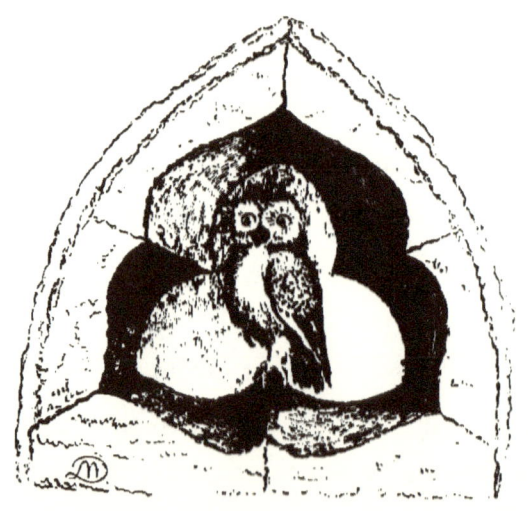

CHAPTER III.

HRISTMAS came, and home came Lord Lovel on his milk-white steed.

The night before the wedding the Baron brought to Ginevra a curiously carved ivory box.

"This is thy mother's wedding gift," said he. "Now is the time to open it."

He took from his purse a small gold key. Ginevra turned the lock. The lid flew up, and showed a heap of strung pearls, each one large as a robin's egg.

"They are beautiful!" exclaimed Ginevra, in delight.

"Beautiful!" echoed Geta.

"Yes," said the Baron. "Their like is not in old England. I bought them at Constantinople, when I was returning from Palestine."

He lifted the long rope, and wound it round his daughter's neck.

"They are fair, my darling," said he, tenderly, "but thy throat is fairer."

Ginevra looked dreamily at the jewel-case; then, turning her eyes inquiringly to her father's, she suddenly asked:

" Was my mother happy?"

" Happy in that she died young," answered the Baron, gloomily.

" Wouldst thou say that of me?" she asked, in wondering sadness.

" No, sweet child. Thou art dear to me as the blood-drops of my heart; and had I as many lives as thou hast hairs on thy head, I would give every one of them for thee, my precious pearl. But no more of this! See, here is thy wedding-ring, my gift to thy mother, engraved with the name of both—Ginevra. I had it from a Jew in Venice. He said it bore a charm, and always brought good fortune to the wearer. And so it has; it has brought me thee."

Ginevra laid the jewels back on the violet velvet lining, and was soon chatting gayly with Geta; but the Baron was restless and uneasy. When he said good-night he strained her to his heart and kissed her again and again, as if it were a last parting; then he doubled the guards of the castle, walked the great hall, and made the grand rounds like one whose anxious thoughts will not let him rest.

Ginevra's quick eye marked the movements of the Baron, and she waited till he rested a moment in his favorite seat by the chimney-corner, and, seating herself on the heavy arm of the oaken chair, she said :

" Is my father troubled to-night ? Tell me what the trouble is, and I may chase it away."

" No, no, little one," answered the Baron, making an effort to smile , " but—"

" But what ? Go on ! What, father ?"

" Only this, dearest. Art thou sure of being perfectly happy ?"

" Entirely sure ; but I could not be if Lovel should take me from thee." She patted his cheek, then touched her blooming mouth to it.

" He will not come between us, child. Nothing on earth, nothing outside of heaven, can do that. But listen, what a fearful night ! How the sea rises, like a fierce beast chained, roaring for its prey ! The coast will show wrecks to-morrow."

"And is it that which makes thee so uneasy, so sorry?"

"No ; but the raging swell, which we hear here as a weak moaning, stirs strange thoughts and brings up strange scenes, vanished long ago. The sea has changing voices. Now as we listen, I hear great guns booming shot and shell, the rush of thousands of feet, the tramp of armies fighting. I loved it when I was a young man ; but it is not the same, because I am not the same. Then it spoke to me of the future ; now it is all of the past. As I hold your dear hand"—he touched the pinky finger-tips to his lips as he spoke—" I am hearing a text my mother taught me (God rest her soul!) : "Boast not thyself of to-morrow."

" But you have not boasted."

" No ; we seem over-confident, and there is a happiness that makes my soul afraid. Look out !"—he pointed to the window—" I thought I saw something pale, a tall shape fly by the window. There ! Now !"

" You might have seen a pale shape half an hour ago in the dusk, where the sun left a little light. It is all black darkness now." She rose, drew aside the curtain, and knelt on the deep window-sill among the roses. " I see nothing but dark. The wind howls like a mad thing in the air, trying locks and bolts to get in. Sad for the poor sailors and their wives waiting at home. Maybe they will never come back, poor things !"

She returned to her place beside the Baron, who looked

silently into the fire; her pretty head drooped on his shoulder, and he leaned his cheek to hers, her hand in his.

" My daughter!" he said, in a tone he never used to aught on earth but her.

" My father!" she answered, softly as a wind-harp sounds.

" I would have my baby once more."

He turned to the maid:

" Geta, go get your mistress ready for bed. Wrap her in my Siberian mantle. She shall rest to-night in the arms which were her first cradle, and I shall rock her to sleep."

Ginevra laughed. " I can easily be a child again. I have only to go a few steps backward," and she disappeared with Geta.

A moment later she was robed in a snow-white mantle which muffled her from head to foot. And, like a wintry fairy, she passed her chamber door, where her father stood waiting. He caught her up from the floor.

' Take care of the baby feet," he said. "These floors are never warm. Thou art all fair, my love. We will not go below. We will sit in the brown parlor."

This was a small room adjoining Ginevra's bedroom, where there was a cumbrous chair, called Prince Rupert's, which was

shaped like a throne. The walls were made strange with portraits
—men in queer costumes looking stiff and ghastly, women rigid
as pasteboard, except the picture of one young girl in long bodice
and flowing skirt, around her hounds and huntsmen, a hawk on
her wrist, her horse at hand ready for mounting—a lovely lady.
This was Ginevra's mother; and she loved the portrait, and always
kept a lamp of perfumed oil burning below it.

The fire was low and ashy in the big fire-place. The Baron
blew a silver whistle, and while waiting for a servant to answer
the call, he kicked together the chunks of logs, sending a train of
fiery sparkles up the chimney.

"Make haste, man!" he said, impatiently. "Heap on the
wood."

The obedient servant piled it from a box like a high, old-fash-
ioned bedstead, which held at least a half cord of logs.

"Quick! quick! What carelessness! This room is cold as
death."

The man went out soon as he could escape, and reported to
the servants that the Baron was in one of his tiger fits. They
wondered why, when he was so pleased over the wedding, and in
their own hall they talked it over with many wonderments.

But the lord of the castle had no dark mood, no tiger fit for Ginevra.

" Now, my darling," said he, holding the light shape across his breast, while he wrapped the fur round her feet, " now I have my little girl all mine own for the last time.   What shall I sing ?"

"About the Norse kings, father.   How they used to steal their brides and sail away over the foaming North seas to the lands of snow and ice."

The Baron was not much of a singer; but the deep roll of his voice well suited the thunder of the storm without.   A strange cradle-song, to be sure, of fighting, of hunting, of blood, and of victory.   An hour passed.   There was no rift in the clouds, no lull in the dismal wind.   Then the snow began to fall—the hushing snow, which seems to quiet heaven and earth.

" It will be fair to-morrow," said Ginevra, sleepily, rousing a little.   " That was a brave song of the pirates.   Now the wind goes down."   She opened the clear blue eyes once more and smiled, showing the pearly little teeth.   " Good-night.   Do not let me tire you, father dear;" and so, murmuring love words her nurse had taught, she went to her innocent dreams—in all the kingdoms of sleep, the sweetest thing that breathed.

It snowed and it snowed and it snowed. Toward morning the castle was a very castle of silence; and the noiseless world lay like a cold white corpse in its cold white shroud.

Ginevra, lapped in downy fur, nested like a bird in her father's breast, and he watched the delicate, upturned face with a watch that knew no weariness, till gray dawn broke over the earth, and the hilltops were tipped with silver.

Many times he touched her feet to feel if they were warm. Many times he leaned his ear to her fragrant breath and softly wound a stray curl of her hair, in rings of gold, round his forefinger. He hummed verses of old tunes some lost love sang in the years long gone, when he was young; and once he whispered a prayer.

Fond, foolish old man! Why wore he the night away in such sad, sweet watching, when there was nothing to make afraid?

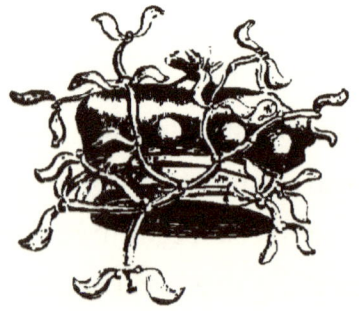

CHAPTER IV.

OVELY was the bride, next day, in her white robe, fastened with golden clasps, every clasp set with an emerald stone; her vest of gold, embroidered with flowers; her floating veil like silver mist, morning blushes on her cheek, and pearls upon her breast. The heavy snow which had fallen in the night did not keep away the wedding guests. They came early in spite of storm and cold. The priest was there; the joy-bells rang; the prayer was said, the blessings given; and never, day nor night, would Lord Lovel part again from Ginevra.

As they sat at the feast, suddenly the bride was missed from the side of her lord. He hastily left the table, and in a few minutes returned and whispered to the Baron.

"'Tis one of her childish plays, a trick only to make a trial of our love," said the Baron, trying to smile. "One more health to Lady Lovel! Fill high the glasses!"

He raised a goblet, but his hand shook; and when he tried to lift the red wine, it poured down the table, like a stream of blood. And soon from guest to guest the panic spread.

"Good friends," he cried, springing to his feet, "there's not a moment to spare. Lady Ginevra is missing—perhaps lost. Lovel, my son, look for her in the main buildings, where I know she is. My Lord of Cranston, with his vassals, will hunt through the south wing. Huntingdon and his followers will search the north wing. Do thou, Ban, go through the vaults and cellars, leaving no stone unturned. Report to me here."

The veins in the Baron's face swelled out like cords; great drops of sweat gathered on his forehead; his lips were pale as ashes. And the brave men around him turned white and trembled. They remembered the prophecy—*the Lady Ginevra is doomed*.

With lighted torches, they scattered to their work. Along the galleries Lovel shouted, " My life, my love, come to me ! Come, or thou art lost !" There was no flying footstep, no ringing laugh, no veil like silver mist, only cold and dark, and the mocking echo, Lost, Lost! When he passed the grand staircase, he felt drawn toward the wall. He thought there was a noise. They listened.

" Be still, Alfred ; I am sure I hear a step," said Lovel, eagerly clasping his hands together, like one in prayer.

" No," said Alfred ; " it is a rat scratching behind the wainscot."

They listened again. Surely something stirred. Hush! They held their breath. A sound nearly like a sob; another; one more; then all was still as the breast when the spirit has fled.

Lovel looked into the tall clock, where she could easily stand upright, behind, under, above it, and found nothing but dust and cobweb. " My lamb, my dove," he cried, " come home, or thou art lost !" Lofty arch and empty distance rang with the sound, but gave back no answer.

Meanwhile, the Baron strode up and down the hall, like a hungry lion in his cage. He looked so awful no one but little Geta dared go near him. Every time the clock struck he would say:

" Geta, is thy Lady's chamber warm ?"

" Warm, my lord."

" And light ?"

" Light, my lord."

" Her slippers by the fire ?"

" Yes, my lord. She would find the bath and all ready, were she here this very minute."

" I would to God she were here, Geta !"

Ah ! bitter chill the night was !   The owl, for all his feathers, was a-cold.   The wind raved and tore at the windows, and sleety snow whirled and hissed and drifted against them, and under the loose old casements.   The Baron groaned in anguish; in this wild storm, where was his tender child the winds of heaven had never visited too roughly?   Where?   Oh ! where ?

At daybreak the companies straggled back.   Not a word was spoken.   The beloved was not found.   They breakfasted on the cold meats of the wedding-feast, and every time a door opened, turned and looked as if to see her dancing home as she had danced away.

Without food or rest, Lord Lovel—oh, how changed !—hunted the highest, the lowest, the loneliest spot, calling her by every dear name.   "Come to me !   Come, or thou art lost !"   And the wind, moaning through black arch and freezing gallery, gave back the echo, Lost !

Four days and nights were wasted thus.   Then they met in the hall, and, in a hoarse, changed voice, the Baron spoke:

" Thanks, my friends, every one.   Be it remembered, he who bringeth me trace of the Lady Ginevra, or clew to her finding, shall have what he may ask, were it half my barony."

Deep lines in his face showed how he had suffered, and his hair, that yesterday was streaked with gray, was white as wool. The wedding guests turned to go, and then the great bell in the tower struck one. There was silence deep as death. Hark! two, three, four; it rang to seventeen. What could it be?

No one inhabited the bell-tower, and, except under orders, the ropes were never touched. That sound, so dread, so solemn, struck on every ear, like a voice from heights beyond the living earth ; the cry of some desolate soul passing through cloudy spaces, the dim region between two worlds. Could it be fairy hands tolling the passing bell for the soul of Ginevra? Was it a ring from heaven that her presence was lost from the abodes of the living, that she must now be numbered with the dead? These questions have not been answered, and will not be answered till the great day comes which ends all question and brings each hidden thing to light.

Till this time the Baron had not shed a tear. When the last sad tone moaned and trembled through the air, he hid his face in his hands, and big drops ran through his fingers, like fast rushing rain.

Children clung to their mothers ; women sobbed together in a crowd ; and warlike men, too brave to be ashamed of tears, fell into each other's arms and cried aloud.

Never were wedding guests like those who that day passed the icy fountain and through the hushing snow of the leafless forest, where the wind was wailing farewell forever, and forever farewell.

From the lonesome hemlocks, loaded with snow, Lovel went back alone to Ginevra's chamber. Garlanded with roses, it was light and warm ; the tiny slippers were before the fire ; her lute, her birds, her needlework, were there ; but the Rose of the World was missing ; missing the little feet that nevermore would lightly run to meet him, nevermore would lightly follow.

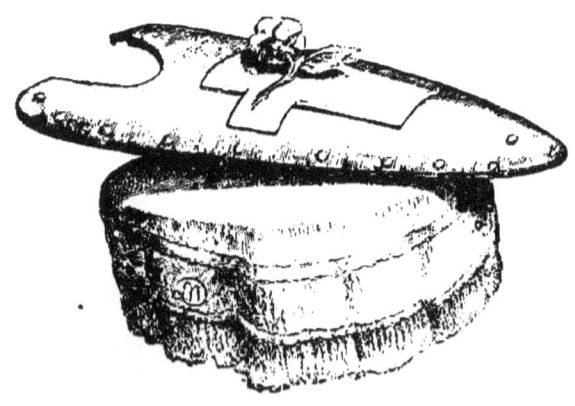

CONCLUSION.

SLOWLY, slowly, days, weeks, and months, went by; and yet the Baron and Lovel searched the castle, now gloomy as a prison. They broke the ice and had the moat dragged; but there were found only the slimy things that swim in still water, and Ban went to the bottom of a deep well in the lowest cellar, and found nothing; nor, from that fatal hour, could anything be guessed, save that Ginevra was not.

Spring came, with birds across the sea; the home wind, the sweet breath of summer brought lilies and violets; the nightingale sang to the roses; but its song could not reach the ear of Ginevra. Lovel wore her picture in his bosom, painted as when last he saw her, laughing and looking back, her finger up, as though she said: "Beware!" The artist caught the very glance of her eye, so winning, yet so arch, it haunts me still, like some wild melody; for I have seen a copy of that self-same picture hanging in the old palace of the Orsini, at Modena.

Many a lady of the land would have walked barefooted to London to win a smile from Lord Lovel; but he never smiled again. His heart was empty as some lone nest clinging to wintry boughs, from which the green leaves have fallen and the singing birds have flown.

With haggard face and sunken eyes he hunted that wide and weary castle, and when a year had gone, he said: "There is no hope. I cannot rest here nor live elsewhere; and so I will throw my life away in battle with the Turk."

The Baron gave him a silver shield and his own sword.

"Take it, my son," said he. "Thou canst try the magic of its blade and strike for Holy Cross; as for me, I shall never mount horse again." Then he leaned on Lovel's neck, and wept sorrowing, knowing they would see each other on earth no more.

In front of battle, Lovel looked death in the face as if he loved it. He fell on the bloody sands of Holy Land, and amid the dead and dying, they buried him where he lay, wrapped in his cloak, his good sword by his side, the sweet picture of his lost love shining on his breast.

Geta and Alfred were married, and the voices of their children were heard as they played about the castle. At Christmas time, when snow whirled through the air, and wind moaned through the halls, they would huddle round the fire, saying to each other: " I hear my Lady's footstep on the stairs;" or, "she is flying through the forest. I see her white robe in the trees. She is coming near, and will call us soon."

Some said Ginevra was spirited away in the storm; some, that a robber from the forest stole her. Many thought her so pure and good the angels had carried her to heaven without dying. But these were idle tales. Where she went none ever knew, nor was she heard of more.

The Baron never rested from his search. All day the old man, wrinkled and bent, groped his way through doleful chambers, and even into the dreadful dungeon, hunting his darling child; and often, at dead of night, his torch flamed through the windows of some far tower, or along the merlons of the dizzy battlements. One day he was found lying on the staircase, her little slippers, yellow and faded, held tightly in his hand. The dull, deep pain was over; the aching feet at rest; his search was ended, never again to begin. They laid him in the vault, among the crumbling bones of his fathers, where he sleeps well.

Years and years and years went by, and the castle stood

empty. It gave no sign of life. The owl and crow were dead, the pavements grown with moss, the rose-garden a waste of weeds. Hangings dropped in rags from black and moldy walls; the draw-bridge rotted in the green and stagnant waters of the moat; the flagstaff fell and went to dust upon the roof; and over all hung a cloud of fear and dread. So it was told something ailed the place—that it was haunted. Nothing stirred the old shadows; they lay like death, year after year; and there were no whisper-ings of warrior or maiden. They were with the still sleepers who dream no dreams.

When a hundred years had passed, the castle was bought by strangers; and one day workmen, repairing the grand staircase, saw a gap in the wall. A secret door had rusted from its hinges, and fallen into a room that looked dark as a grave.

There stood an old oak chest, worm-eaten and mildewed, its iron bands coated with rust, and a light-hearted girl, young and thoughtless as Ginevra, said : " Let us take it from this place, and see what it holds."

The workmen slowly dragged it toward the light, but on the way it fell, it burst ; and lo, a skeleton ! Around its head, to which the golden hair yet clung, a coronet of pearls ; here and there an emerald stone in a clasp holding shreds of gold, and in the dust that once had been a hand, a wedding-ring engraved— "GINEVRA."

> " There, then, had she found a grave!
>   Within that chest had she concealed herself,
>   Fluttering with joy, the happiest of the happy,
>   When a spring-lock, that lay in ambush there,
>   Fastened her down forever!"

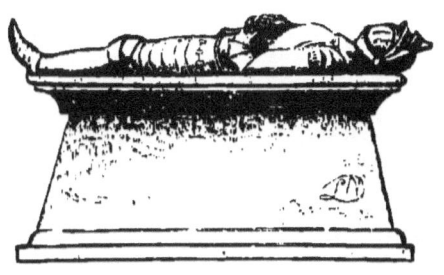

ANOTHER VERSION IN POETRY
OF GINEVRA.

THE MISTLETOE BOUGH.

THE mistletoe hung in the castle hall,
The holly bright shone on the old oak wall,
The Baron's retainers were blithe and gay,
While keeping their Christmas holiday.
The Baron beheld with a father's pride
His beautiful child, young Lovel's bride ;
And she, with her bright eye, seemed to be
The star of that goodly companie.

  O the mistletoe bough ! O the mistletoe bough !

" I'm weary of dancing, now," she cried,
" Here tarry a moment, I'll hide, I'll hide ;
And, Lovel, be sure thou art first to trace
The clue to my secret lurking-place."

Away she ran, and her friends began
Each tower to search, each nook to scan ;
And young Lovel cried, " O where dost thou hide ?
I'm lonesome without thee, my own dear bride."
     O the mistletoe bough ! O the mistletoe bough !

They sought her that night, they sought her next day,
They sought her in vain till a week passed away ;
The highest, the lowest, the loneliest spot,
Young Lovel sought wildly, but found her not.
And years flew by, and their grief at last
Was told as a sorrowful tale long past.
When Lovel appeared the children cried,
"See the old man weeps for his fairy bride."
     O the mistletoe bough ! O the mistletoe bough !

At length an old chest, which had long lain hid,
Was found in the castle ; they raised the lid.
The skeleton form lay mouldering there,
In the bridal wreath of the lady fair.

O sad was her fate when in sportive jest
She hid from her lord in the old oak chest ;
It closed with a spring, and her bridal bloom
Lay withering there in a lonely tomb.
    O the mistletoe bough ! O the mistletoe bough !

THE FAMOUS POEM GINEVRA.

BY

SAMUEL ROGERS.

Saml Rogers.

GINEVRA.

BY SAMUEL ROGERS.

IF thou shouldst ever come by choice or chance
To MODENA, where still religiously
Among her ancient trophies is preserved
BOLOGNA's bucket (in its chain it hangs
Within that reverend tower, the Guirlandine),
Stop at a Palace near the Reggio-gate,
Dwelt in of old by one of the ORSINI.
Its noble gardens, terrace above terrace,
And rich in fountains, statues, cypresses,
Will long detain thee; thro' their arched walks,
Dim at noonday, discovering many a glimpse
Of knights and dames, such as in old romance,
And lovers, such as in heroic song,
Perhaps the two, for groves were their delight,
Who in the spring-time, as alone they sat,
Venturing together on a tale of love,

Read only part that day.*——A summer-sun
Sets ere one half is seen ; but ere thou go,
Enter the house—prythee, forget it not—
And look awhile upon a picture there.

'Tis of a Lady in her earliest youth,
The very last of that illustrious race,
Done by ZAMPIERI †—but by whom I care not.
He who observes it—ere he passes on,
Gazes his fill, and comes and comes again,
That he may call it up when far away.

She sits, inclining forward as to speak,
Her lips half-open and her finger up,
As tho' she said " Beware !" Her vest of gold
Broidered with flowers, and clasped from head to foot,
An emerald-stone in every golden clasp ;
And on her brow, fairer than alabaster,
A coronet of pearls. But then her face,
So lovely, yet so arch, so full of mirth,
The overflowings of an innocent heart—

---

* Inferno. V.   † Commonly called DOMENICHINO.

GINEVRA; OR, THE OLD OAK CHEST.

It haunts me still, tho' many a year has fled,
Like some wild melody!
              Alone it hangs
Over a mouldering heir-loom, its companion,
An oaken chest, half-eaten by the worm,
But richly carved by ANTONY of Trent
With scripture-stories from the Life of Christ;
A chest that came from VENICE, and had held
The ducal robes of some old Ancestor.
That, by the way—it may be true or false—
But don't forget the picture; and thou wilt not,
When thou hast heard the tale they told me there.

  She was an only child; from infancy
The joy, the pride of an indulgent Sire.
Her Mother dying of the gift she gave,
That precious gift, what else remained to him?
The young GINEVRA was his all in life,
Still as she grew, forever in his sight;
And in her fifteenth year became a bride,
Marrying an only son, FRANCESCO DORIA,
Her playmate from her birth, and her first love.

Just as she looks there in her bridal dress,
She was all gentleness, all gaiety ;
Her pranks the favourite theme of every tongue.
But now the day was come, the day, the hour :
Now, frowning, smiling, for the hundredth time,
The nurse, that ancient lady, preached decorum ;
And, in the lustre of her youth, she gave
Her hand, with her heart in it, to FRANCESCO.

Great was the joy ; but at the Bridal feast,
When all sat down, the Bride was wanting there.
Nor was she to be found !   Her Father cried,
"'Tis but to make a trial of our love !"
And filled his glass to all ; but his hand shook,
And soon from guest to guest the panic spread.
'Twas but that instant she had left FRANCESCO,
Laughing and looking back and flying still,
Her ivory-tooth imprinted on his finger.
But now, alas, she was not to be found ;
Nor from that hour could anything be guessed,
But that she was not !

             Weary of his life,

Francesco flew to Venice, and forthwith
Flung it away in battle with the Turk.
Orsini lived ; and long might'st thou have seen
An old man wandering as in quest of something,
Something he could not find—he knew not what.
When he was gone, the house remained awhile
Silent and tenantless—then went to strangers.

   Full fifty years were past, and all forgot,
When on an idle day, a day of search
'Mid the old lumber in the Gallery,
That mouldering chest was noticed ; and 'twas said
By one as young, as thoughtless as Ginevra,
" Why not remove it from its lurking-place ? "
'Twas done as soon as said ; but on the way
It burst, it fell ; and lo, a skeleton,
With here and there a pearl, an emerald-stone,
A golden clasp, clasping a shred of gold.
All else had perished—save a nuptial ring,
And a small seal, her mother's legacy,
Engraven with a name, the name of both—
" Ginevra."

There then had she found a grave !
Within that chest had she concealed herself,
Fluttering with joy, the happiest of the happy ;
When a spring-lock, that lay in ambush there,
Fastened her down forever !

www.ingramcontent.com/pod-product-compliance
Lightning Source LLC
Chambersburg PA
CBHW030009030726
47499CB00008B/2977

* 9 7 8 3 7 4 3 4 1 7 9 8 4 *